The ~~Amazing~~ Odorous Adventures of Stinky Dog

Tales from the House of Bunnicula Books by James Howe:

It Came from Beneath the Bed!
Invasion of the Mind Swappers from Asteroid 6!
Howie Monroe and the Doghouse of Doom
Screaming Mummies of the Pharaoh's Tomb II
Bud Barkin, Private Eye
The ~~Amazing~~ Odorous Adventures of Stinky Dog

Other Bunnicula Books by James Howe:
Bunnicula (with Deborah Howe)
Howliday Inn
The Celery Stalks at Midnight
Nighty-Nightmare
Return to Howliday Inn
Bunnicula Strikes Again!

Bunnicula and Friends Books by James Howe:
The Vampire Bunny
Hot Fudge

James Howe is the author of the award-winning best-seller *Bunnicula* and its sequels, as well as many other popular books for young readers, including *The Misfits* and the Pinky and Rex series for younger readers. He lives in New York State.

TALES FROM THE HOUSE OF BUNNICULA

The Amazing Odorous Adventures of Stinky Dog

JAMES HOWE

ILLUSTRATED BY BRETT HELQUIST

Aladdin Paperbacks
NEW YORK LONDON TORONTO SYDNEY

First Aladdin Paperbacks edition September 2004

Text copyright © 2003 by James Howe
Illustrations copyright © 2003 by Brett Helquist

ALADDIN PAPERBACKS
An imprint of Simon & Schuster
Children's Publishing Division
1230 Avenue of the Americas
New York, NY 10020

Also available in an Atheneum Books for Young Readers hardcover edition.
Designed by Ann Bobco
The text of this book was set in Berkeley.
The illustrations were rendered in acrylics and oils.

Manufactured in the United States of America
10 9 8 7 6 5 4 3

The Library of Congress has cataloged the hardcover edition as follows:
Howe, James, 1946–
The Amazing Odorous Adventures of Stinky Dog / James Howe; illustrated by Brett Helquist.
p. cm.—(Tales from the House of Bunnicula, #6)
Summary: Under a deadline from his editor, Howie the wirehaired dachshund creates a story featuring a superhero whose ability to stink enables him and his sidekick, a sparrow named Little D, to fight crime in Central City.
ISBN-13: 978-0-689-85633-4 (hc.)
ISBN-10: 0-689-85633-4 (hc.)
[1. Authorship—Fiction. 2. Heroes—Fiction. 3. Dachshunds—Fiction. 4. Dogs—Fiction. 5. Humorous stories.] I. Helquist, Brett, ill. II. Title. III. Series: Howe, James, 1946-
Tales from the House of Bunnicula, #6.
PZ7. H83727 Am 2003
[Fic.]—dc21   2003001661
ISBN-13: 978-0-689-87412-3 (pbk.)
ISBN-10: 0-689-87412-X (pbk.)

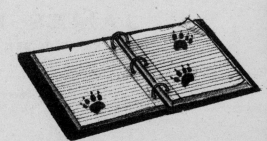

Life is even better than fiction—especially when you have a sweet stinky dog like our Betsy. This book is for her.
—J. H.

For Mary Jane
—B. H.

The ~~Amazing~~ Odorous Adventures of Stinky Dog

HOWIE'S WRITING JOURNAL

I am so upset I can't write! Well, okay, I
can write, but I can't write a <u>book</u>! I owe my
editor another book <u>soon</u>, and I don't even
have an idea. I don't think my editor would
be very happy to get a book about how I
just had my third bath in three days!

You would think—what with his being a
college professor and her being a lawyer
and all—that Mr. and Mrs. Monroe would be

smart enough to figure out that a dog isn't a dog without certain smells in his life.

But do they say, "Oh, Howie, what is that delightful aroma—a new aftershave?"

Nooooo. They say, "P. U.! Howie, you stink! Have you been rolling around in the compost heap again? Now you're going to have to have another bath."

Then they tell me that the pile of garbage and rotting food and smelly weeds in the far corner of the yard is there to make fertilizer for their garden. Fine. I have nothing against fertilizer.

In fact, I'm all for fertilizer. But how come _they_ get to enjoy it and Uncle Harold and I _don't_?

Life is so unfair.

Especially when you're a dog.

I'm going up to Toby's room to sulk. Maybe a good sulk will clear my head so I can come up with an idea for my next book.

Oh, the curse of the writer's life! Readers demand more books. Editors give you contracts, then insist that you actually _write_ the books you promised you would. But what of the poor writer? Is he a machine, churning out books as if they were nothing more than chew bones or squeaky toys? (Not that I have anything against chew bones or squeaky toys.) Or is he a living, breathing creature made of flesh and blood who can't be expected to create when he's been scolded (again) for rolling around in the compost heap and made to suffer the indignity of three baths in three days!?

Life is so unfair.

Especially when you're a dog.

And a writer.

HOWIE'S WRITING JOURNAL

The best thing just happened! Toby was in his room, reading this big stack of comic books, and he must have known how I was feeling because he said, "Come on up here, boy, and let me read to you."

So I did, and he did, and now I know what I'm going to write!

The ~~Amazing~~ Odorous Adventures of Stinky Dog

By Howie Monroe

CHAPTER 1:
"TROUBLE IN CENTER CITY"

Things were bad in Center City. Gangs roamed the streets, knocking little old ladies down and running off with their handbags. Signs were posted everywhere:

> **WANTED:**
> **GANGS CARRYING HANDBAGS**
> **MAY BE DANGEROUS**

No one was safe. Not even dogs. Dogs were not allowed to be smelly. If they were, they were locked up in the jug. The can. The cooler. The hoosegow.

People kept their little old ladies indoors and gave their dogs baths every day. Sometimes more than once.

It was a terrible time.

Howie Monroe, a decent, mild-mannered, and law-abiding citizen of Center City, worried about the safety of his family, the Monroes, even though they gave him too many baths and would not let him roll around in their compost heap. ~~Why have a compost heap, he wanted to know, if you can't roll around in~~

Howie wished there was something he could do to make life better in Center City, but what *could* he do? After all, he was only one small dachshund in a world gone mad, one tiny voice in a sea of voices, one pebble in a field of boulders, one itsy-bitsy minnow in a school of sharks! He didn't even dare leave his house for fear that, unable to resist the lure of the compost heap, he would be picked up for unlawful stinkiness and tossed into the clink where he'd have to share a cell with gangs of criminals armed with handbags.

One day he was sleeping under the coffee table when he was awakened by a loud *KEERASHHH* from outside. Harold and Chester, the other decent, mild-mannered (except Chester, sometimes), and law-abiding pets with whom he shared his home, came running into the room.

9

"What was that?" Chester the cat cried out in alarm.

"It sounded like KEERASHHH to me!" said the keenly aware dachshund puppy.

"Let's investigate," said Harold.

They all jumped up onto the sofa and peered out from behind the living room curtains.

Howie couldn't believe his ever-observant eyes. A large garbage truck had KEERASHHHed into the fire hydrant (his *favorite* fire hydrant, too, but never mind) in front of the house. Garbage was tumbling out of the truck while water sprayed through it, turning it into a big, gooey, soupy, smelly mess.

"It's every dog's dream!" Howie said, gasping.

"It's going to have to remain just that," Harold, the older and more sensible dog, said with a sigh. "A dream."

"But why?" Howie, the younger and more impulsive (not to mention impetuous and spontaneous) puppy, demanded to know, even though he already did. Know.

"The mayor of Center City hates smelly dogs," Harold reminded him.

"That's not fair!" cried the outspoken and righteous Howie. "We've got to do something about it!"

"There's nothing to be done," Harold said.

"Center City is full of corruption and crime," said Chester. "It will take somebody a lot more powerful than a mere mortal to do anything about it, Howie."

Howie scowled. He hated feeling power-less. Even worse, he hated feeling mere.

Whatever that was.

"Maybe I *can* do something about it!" cried the brave, courageous, and defiant pup. "Maybe I'll just go out there and roll around in that muck. I'd like to see somebody try and stop me!"

"No!" cried Harold. "You'll end up in the slammer, boy! You don't want to break your mother's heart!"

Howie sniffed back a tear. "My mother raised me to follow my conscience," Howie told the older dog. "She would be proud of me!"

Harold sniffed back a tear himself. "You're right," he said. "It takes a young fellow like yourself to remind old fellows like Chester and me that there's more to bravery than being brave. Sometimes there's being stupid."

"Right on!" Howie asserted.

SKREEEE—he ran as fast as his little legs would carry him until **KAPLOOMPH**—he shoved through the pet door and—**PLIPPITY PLOPPITY PLIPPITY PLOPPITY**—he charged around the yard until he reached the front curb and—**SHHPLOOFFF**—he threw himself into the soggy mess of garbage and waited for the coppers to arrive.

It didn't take long. **ZEEHEE ZEE-HEEZEEHEE** came the sound of the sirens. Howie Monroe braced himself. He was about to be arrested! He was going to spend the rest of his days in the Big House eating gruel and fearing handbags!

And that's just what would have happened if it hadn't been for the sudden storm that sent a bolt of lightning—*ZZ^{ZZ}ZAPPP*—right to the hydrant next to Howie's back left leg. That bolt of lightning changed everything—not just for the decent, mild-mannered, and law-abiding Howie Monroe . . . not just for all the Monroes . . . not just for Center City . . . but for the **ENTIRE UNIVERSE**!

HOWIE'S WRITING JOURNAL

AWESOME! Howie Monroe is going to be a superhero! I always knew I had it in me to be larger than life.

Uncle Harold likes what I wrote so far, although he said he isn't sure he cares for the way I'm portraying him and Pop. (Pop is what I call Chester in real life.)

He said, "<u>old</u> <u>fellows</u>?"

I waited for him to make his point.

He also said I'm using too many adjectives again (poor Uncle Harold), and he thinks my readers won't know what some of them mean—like "impetuous," for example.

I said, "That's okay. I don't know what some of them mean either. Like 'impetuous,' for example."

Then he asked why I keep using words like "can" and "slammer" and "hoosegow" when I could just say "jail."

I said, "Uncle Harold, have you ever heard of a thesaurus?"

"Yes, Howie," he said.

"Well, I found one on the floor next to Mr. Monroe's desk, and it is so cool. Do you know how it works?"

"Yes, Howie," he repeated. "It gives you lists of words with the same or similar meanings for the word you look up. That doesn't mean, however, that you have to use <u>all</u> the words, including ones you don't understand. And you certainly don't have to use all of them in the same chapter."

Honestly. Uncle Harold is such a fussy-boots sometimes.

Doesn't he want writing to be <u>fun</u>?

CHAPTER 2:
"THE BIRTH OF STINKY DOG"

ZZZZVVTZZZ! ZZZNGG! ZZZBBEEZZOOM!
Waves of electricity shot through Howie's garbage-encrusted body! His hairs stood on end! His eyeballs went **BOINGA-BOINGA-BOINGA!** **BOINGA-**

Suddenly Howie Monroe was no longer just a cute, adorable, and normal-smelling wire-haired dachshund puppy (although he was still cute and adorable). Suddenly, thanks to

18

a bolt of lightning and a fateful combination of garbage and H_2O, Howie Monroe was bestowed with the gift of incredible **SUPER-STENCH**! Suddenly, Howie Monroe was **STINKY DOG**, the stinkiest dog alive!

(No one knew this, of course. All anyone knew was that Howie Monroe smelled *baaaaaaaaad*!)

"Whew!" the first policeman said as he jumped out of his patrol car. "That is one smelly—"

He keeled over before he could finish the sentence.

"Frankie! You okay, Frankie?" A second law enforcement agent jumped out of the car. He, too, was hit by a wall of stinkiness.

"Man, what is that stench?" he asked, holding his nose. "I've never smelled anything like it! It's malodorous . . . it's miasmic . . . it's . . ."

"Look, Sarge, over there by the hydrant," called a third gendarme. "It's . . . it's a stinky dog!"

"That's no ordinary stinky dog," said the police sergeant who was holding his nose.

"But what else could it be, Sarge?"

"It's foul . . . it's fetid . . . it's the rankest compound of villainous smell that ever offended nostril!"

"Wow," said the other copper, who, right before he passed out, thought how cool it was that Sarge could quote Shakespeare straight out of the thesaurus.

The constable who was called Sarge inched his way toward Howie.

"Paws up!" he commanded.

"Catch!" the clever and fast-thinking super-hero wirehaired dachshund puppy replied, tossing a rotting head of cabbage at the police officer.

Without thinking, Sarge let go of his nose. "I'm undone!" he cried.

KEE-FWAPP! He fell over backward, landing in a pile of reeking and rancid, not to mention repulsive, refuse.

"All right!" said Howie. He started thinking about all the great smells around him when an amazing thing happened.

ZHHVVOOOVVOOMMMM! A whole bunch of gases formed under Howie's formerly merely mortal, but now superheroic, tushy and made a vaporous propulsion of fumes. He was being lifted up, up, up! He was flying!

"*Yes!*" Howie, aka Stinky Dog, cried out. "I've always wanted to fly, but not if it meant having to be a bird, because birds eat worms, which is totally gross. Not only that, birds go to the bathroom while they're flying, which is even more gross. In fact, other than feathers and flying, I can't think of anything that isn't gross about birds. Well, some of them make nice noises. If you like that sort of thing. I mean, a tweet isn't in the same league as a bark, but still—"

Luckily for the interest of the reader, Howie, aka Stinky Dog, was distracted from his thoughts by a cry for help.

"Help! Help! Someone is stealing my handbag!"

Faster than you could say, "Get the air freshener!" Stinky Dog was on the job!

ZOOOOOOOM!

Stinky Dog flew through the air and landed with a loud *THUHDD*!

"Stop!" he commanded in a superheroic voice. "Cease! Desist! Halt! Cut it out! Have done!"

Right in front of him, right there on the streets of Center City, where you'd normally figure you were safe (but that was before evil and corruption had seeped into every pore of the . . . something), right there before his very eyes, a crime was taking place!

The criminals were a couple of sleazy-looking characters whose pictures were probably plastered on every post office wall from here to Sacramento. They had the little old lady in a headlock and were about to separate her handbag from her person with the aid of a pair of purple scissors that looked like they'd been stolen out of a kindergarten classroom. What kind of villainous, low-life, miserable, rotten, wicked, kindergarten-scissors-stealing bad eggs were these? The law-breaking kind, that's what!

"This bag has my life savings in it!" the little old lady cried. "Please, kind stranger who flew down from the sky, don't let them take it!"

Stinky Dog regarded the thugs with disgust. "Let her go or I'll blow your nostrils from here to Sacramento!" he shouted.

The two toughs laughed.

"You and who else?" one of them snarled.

"Yeah, what kind of superhero are you supposed to be, anyway?" the other said, trying to decide whether he should jeer or sneer (or maybe scoff). "You don't even have an outfit."

"An outfit?" asked Stinky Dog.

"A cape. A pair of form-fitting trousers with little panty-things and a big letter on your chest."

For a moment Stinky Dog felt downhearted, discouraged, and deflated. Then he remembered:

27

He *was* wearing an outfit! They just couldn't see it. But they would *smell* it soon enough!

He took a step toward them, then another, then another until—**ACKKKKK!**—the hooligans released the little old lady and clutched at their own throats.

"What is that horrible emanation?" one of them cried before he hit the sidewalk with a loud **SHPWOP**.

"Bruce!" the other one cried. "What's the matter, Bruce?"

The one named Bruce managed to croak, "Get to B-Man, Carl. Tell him, tell him—"

But Bruce couldn't finish. He was knocked out by **SUPER-STENCH**!

Carl looked back up over his shoulder. Stinky Dog was coming closer.

"*Nooooo!*" the remaining roughneck roared, reaching to take hold of his nose. But it was too late.

ACKKKKK! SHPHOP!

"You saved me!" cried the little old lady, who began searching through her bag to make sure her life savings were still there. "Here, let me give you a little something for your kindness." She handed Stinky Dog a chew bone.

"Thank you, ma'am," said Stinky Dog modestly and humbly, not to mention politely.

He would have stayed to make conversation and enjoy his chew bone, but a far-off sound caught his attention.

"I think I'm needed elsewhere, ma'am," he said.

He closed his eyes, thought stinky thoughts, and—*ZHHVVOOOVVOOMMMM!*—he was flying through the air to his next adventure!

Howie's Writing Journal

Uncle Harold taught me a new word. He said that I did a great job of "alliteration" when I wrote "the remaining roughneck roared."

I didn't get what he was talking about at first. I said, "Uncle Harold, I am not guilty of alliteration. You know it's wrong to litter."

He said, "'Alliteration' means repeating the same sound—usually a consonant—at the beginning of two or more words in a row. It's a style thing."

Wow. I did a style thing without even knowing it.

I wonder what "consonant" means.

It would have been nice if Uncle Harold could have complimented me and left it at that. But, no, he had to go on. "One thing bothers me," he said. "Why didn't the little old lady pass out from Stinky Dog's stinkiness? The two criminals did."

Well, am I supposed to know _everything_?

He said the reader would want to know.

Sigh. Readers can be such a nuisance.

Nothing personal.

Fine. I'll fix it later. Right now, I want to get to Stinky Dog's next adventure.

CHAPTER 4:
"P. U. TO THE TWENTIETH POWER"

CHUGGA-CHUGGA-CHUGGA-CHUGGA! OOOOOORRRRROOOOO!

To the ordinary pair of ears, it sounded like nothing more than an ordinary train on an ordinary day, making its ~~ordinary~~ usual, normal, and customary way to the Center City train station, but to super ears like those belonging to Stinky Dog, it was the sound of a train in trouble.

Propelled by a jet stream of wickedly smellful fumes, Stinky Dog surveyed the landscape below him. "What a great view!" he said to a passing bird, who said *tweet* in response and then went to the bathroom.

"That is so gross," Stinky Dog commented.

"You're calling *me* gross?" said the bird. "Try getting downwind of yourself and see who's gross."

Stinky Dog never knew birds could be sarcastic.

OOOOOORRRRROOOOO
SKREEEEEEEEEEEEEEEEEEE!

"There!" the bird shouted. He would introduce himself later as Dean.

"I'm on it!" said Stinky Dog, letting the bird know who was in charge. "Look! The train is going to go off the tracks! We've got to do something!"

"But what *can* we do?" asked the bird. "I am only one small sparrow in a world gone mad, one tiny voice in a sea of voices, one—"

"We don't have time for that!" Stinky Dog snapped. "We've got to save the people on that train!"

With eyesight as sharp as the black key above middle C on a finely tuned concert piano, he was able to make out a piece of bent rail. If he didn't get to it fast, the train would go off the track and . . .

The terrible unspoken rest of that sentence hardened his resolve as he took a nosedive straight for the bent rail and thought incredibly stinky thoughts.

"P. U. to the twentieth power!" he heard the bird say behind him.

Who cared what a stupid bird had to say? He might have smelled like the world's biggest compost heap, but it was working! Waves of **SUPER-STENCH** passed through the air, making their way to the rail below him.

Wow! Stinky Dog thought as he watched the steel melt and mold itself back to the original track seconds before the train passed over it. The passengers were safe!

Maybe that bird wasn't so stupid, after all. It *was* P. U. to the twentieth power! The odorousness (or pungency) (or effluvium) was so great that it actually created heat—heat that was strong enough to bend steel!

"That was awesome, stinky dog," said the

bird. "Can you teach me how to do that?"

"I don't think so," said the flying wire-haired dachschund puppy, who was only slighted winded after his heroic effort. "And how did you know my name?"

"I didn't."

"You called me Stinky Dog."

"That's what you are."

"Well, it's also my name. I'm Stinky Dog. I'm a superhero. Who are you?"

"I'm Dean," said the bird. "I'm a sparrow."

And thus a great friendship was formed.

HOWIE'S WRITING JOURNAL

Oh, swell. I let my friend Delilah read what I've written so far, and all she had to say was, "It's all about boys! One helpless little old lady. That's your only female character."

"It's a superhero story," I reminded her.

"So? Girls can be superheroes! Look at Wonder Woman and Batgirl and Xena."

I have no idea how Delilah knows these

things. Sometimes she is too informed for her own good.

Or for my own good, anyway.

"Fine," I told her, "I'll bring a girl into the story."

"And she'd better not be helpless," Delilah said.

"Fine," I said.

Do all writers go through this? Why can't I just write what I _want_ to write? I don't know _how_ to bring a girl character into this story without her being helpless. I mean, there isn't room for two superheroes—and

I want to be the superhero! Delilah is always butting in and telling me what to do.

The thing is, I like Delilah and I don't want her to be mad at me. Maybe she has a point. I'll think about it.

Okay, I thought about it. I'm not sure she has a point.

CHAPTER 5:
"STINKY DOG AND LITTLE D"

SKKKRREEEEEEEECCHHH!

PHOOFPH!

The train came to a halt. People were running back down the tracks toward Stinky Dog and Dean.

Think fragrant thoughts, Stinky Dog told himself. He had figured out how his powers worked. *If I think aromatic thoughts,* he told himself, *no one will get hurt. Think sweet, perfumy, ambrosial thoughts. Rose gardens, spring rain, powdered baby bottoms.*

People were cheering as they came closer.

"You saved us!" the train conductor cried.

"Who are you, mysterious stranger who flew down from the sky?" shouted a newspaper reporter who happened to be on the train.

Suddenly a new thought occurred to Stinky Dog! Maybe it wouldn't be such a good idea to let others get close enough that they could discover his true identity. Who knew what problems it might cause the Monroes if it was known they were harboring a stinky dog—a heroic stinky dog, but a stinky dog nonetheless. As everyone knew, it was illegal to be a stinky dog in Center City.

Before the approaching crowd could get too close, he reversed his thoughts. *Rotting apples, dead fish, dirty diapers.*

ZOOOOOOOM! He was out of there!

"That was cool," said Dean, who was flying at his side. "Maybe we should come up with some outfits to disguise ourselves." Beneath them, the crowd was yelling. Shouting. Crying out. Raising a clamor. Vociferating.

"We?" said Howie over the rapidly receding ruckus. (Or was it the distantly diminishing din?)

"*Please* let me be your sidekick," said Dean. "I want to be larger than life, too."

"You're a sparrow," Stinky Dog pointed out.

"Not everyone can be an eagle," Dean replied. "Even sparrows yearn to soar."

Stinky Dog nodded earnestly and thought-fully, not to mention pensively. Dean was right. Besides, with writing like that, Howie Monroe might have a chance of winning the Newbony Award.

"I don't *have* to be larger than life if you don't want me to be," the persistent bird went on. "I can be small and still be a superhero's sidekick. You could call me Little D."

The steadfast sparrow was growing on Stinky Dog. He thought, *A superhero's life can be a lonely life. It would be nice to have some company.*

"Little D," he said. "Let's go make us some outfits."

HOWIE'S WRITING JOURNAL

Uncle Harold asked me how come Dean can smell Stinky Dog and not pass out.

I told him, "Uncle Harold, Stinky Dog flies through the air. If every bird he comes near passes out, the ground will be covered with passed-out birds before you can say, 'watch out below.'"

I ran out of room before he could ask any more pesky questions.

Meanwhile, using a thesaurus is exhausting. Who knew there were so many <u>words</u>?

I'll bet the Newbony Award committee loves stuff like "vociferating" and "rapidly receding ruckus," though. Not to mention "Even sparrows yearn to soar."

Years from now (or maybe next year), I'll be signing autographs after winning the Newbony Award and people will say, "Isn't your paw getting tired?" And I'll say, "You think this is something? You should have seen how tired my paw got using the thesaurus!" Then we'll all have a good laugh.

(I wonder if my paw will get tired.)

CHAPTER 6:
"MAKING THE WORLD
SAFE FOR STINKINESS"

WHIRRR! **ZZZZZ!** **DING-DING-DING!**
WHIRRRRRRR!

The sound of the sewing machine meant only one thing: Stinky Dog and Little D were making themselves some outfits. Everyone wondered how a dog and a bird knew how to operate a sewing machine, but they didn't take into account that a) Stinky Dog was a superhero with superheroic powers, and b) ever since Martha

51

Stewart came on the scene, who *didn't* know how to sew outfits or make charming yet functional sectional sofas out of used milk cartons?

Pretty soon they had capes and form-fitting trousers and little panty-things and big letters on their chests. And masks. No one would recognize them now.

"Look! Up in the sky!"

"It's Stinky Dog and Little D!"

Well, okay, everybody recognized them, but no one knew their true identities.

Not even Howie's friends Harold, Chester, and Delilah.

"Did you see today's paper?" Harold asked one morning after breakfast. "Stinky Dog saved a group of schoolchildren from a cave-in!"

Chester chimed in, "Yesterday Stinky Dog and his sidekick, Little D, stopped seventeen attempted robberies and rescued twenty-four dogs who were about to be arrested for stinkiness."

"I wonder who Stinky Dog and Little D are," Delilah said with a sigh.

Howie and Dean winked at each other.

Chester said, "We may never know. They're too fast, speedy, and quick to be caught. Not to mention cagey, sly, and elusive."

"There's only one power great enough to match theirs," Harold said mysteriously.

"Do you mean the mayor of Center City?" Howie asked.

"The mayor of Center City is small potatoes

compared to the one I'm talking about," said Harold enigmatically.

"Then who are you talking about?"

"Whom."

"Who's Hoom?"

"Not 'Whose whom.' *Whom* are you talking about?"

"Are we talking about Hoom? Who's Hoom?"

"Whom . . . oh, never mind. What I'm trying to say is, I am talking about B-Man."

"B-Man, B-Man, where have I heard that name before?" Howie mused. Dean kicked him in the shins, which Howie barely felt since Dean was only a bird, although he felt it enough to realize what Dean was trying to tell him: *Hush up about that! You heard about B-Man when you were Stinky Dog!*

"I've never told you about B-Man, Howie," Harold went on, unaware of and also oblivious to what Howie had just said, "because I wanted to protect you. I thought you were too young, but perhaps the time has come. B-Man is—"

KEERASHHH!

"Sounds like trouble!" said Dean. "We'd better—"

It was Howie's turn to kick Dean in the shins. Or whatever passes for shins on birds. "Um, we'll be right back, we just—"

Luckily for Howie and Dean, the others weren't paying attention. They had jumped up onto the sofa to see what was happening outside. Howie and Dean made a mad dash for the kitchen where they changed into their superhero outfits (which they'd hidden behind the refrigerator), rushed out the back door, and thought stinky thoughts. Soon they were up, up, and away, and people were shouting, "Look! Up in the sky!" "It's a bird!" "It's a dog!" "It's a bird *and* a dog!"

It went on like this for weeks. The jails filled up with criminals, handbags were returned to their rightful owners, and petitions circulated asking that dogs be allowed to roll around in compost heaps and smell to their hearts' content. Stinky Dog and Little D were making the world a safer, happier, and stinkier place in which to live.

The only problem was that Howie had to listen to Harold and Chester wonder about Stinky Dog's true identity, never guessing that he was none other than their very own modest, humble, yet daring and courageous, friend. What was worse was having to listen to Delilah, who had always thought Howie was the coolest thing since chew bones and now couldn't stop talking about Stinky Dog.

"Why can't *you* be like Stinky Dog?" she would say. "He's always rescuing damsels in distress. Why can't he rescue *me*?"

Little did Delilah know that soon she would get her wish.

HOWIE'S WRITING JOURNAL

Writing is for the birds!

(No offense, Dean.)

(I just remembered Dean isn't real.)

(Writing is confusing.)

Anyway, there I was feeling all proud of myself for the way I kept Harold from revealing the true identity of B-Man (since it's too early in the story). Then I showed Uncle Harold and Delilah what I just wrote, and did they say, "Great job!" or "Way to go, Writer Dog!"

No!

Uncle Harold said, "It doesn't make sense that Harold and Chester wouldn't know the true identity of Stinky Dog. Weren't they watching out the window when Howie was transformed by the bolt of lightning?"

To which I said, "Well, maybe they got scared and jumped off the sofa and weren't watching anymore."

"Your readers don't know that," Uncle Harold said.

"They do now!" I told him.

Uncle Harold gave me one of his looks as if to say that including important details in my writing journal instead of in the story itself is cheating or something. I seriously think he needs to go lighten up.

And he should take Delilah with him when he does.

She was so angry she could hardly talk. Let's see, I think what she said was, "Can't write female characters." "Making me sound like a ninny." "Wouldn't know a female super-hero if one fell on you." Stuff like that.

I probably shouldn't have let her read the last chapter. She doesn't know I have a plan for Delilah's character.

I actually have a plan for the whole rest of the book.

I even know who B-Man is.

It's cool having a plan.

It also involves a lot of thinking.

I may need to lie down for a little while.

CHAPTER 7:
"SO WE MEET AT LAST, B-MAN!"

One day Howie and Dean were sitting around chewing the fat. (That's just an expression. Neither of them chewed fat. It means they were shooting the breeze, talking, having a little chat. In fact, Howie was chewing a chew bone and Dean was chewing a sesame seed he'd found on the sidewalk outside a bagel store. Dean could get as much enjoyment from chewing a sesame seed as Howie got from chewing a chew bone.) (Well, almost as much.)

"What do you think will happen to us today, Big D?" Dean asked. (Dean had taken to calling Howie Big D, as in D-for-Dog, since he was Little D. Howie didn't object. He was a dachshund. He'd waited his whole life for someone to look up to him.)

"Who knows?" Howie, aka Big D, aka Stinky Dog, answered. "That's one of the exciting things about being a superhero—"

"And a superhero's sidekick," Dean said.

Howie smiled at him. "Right," he said. "You never know—"

SSSHHPLLOOSH! SSHHK-WUMPSH! SSSMMURRRSHHH!

Dean dropped his half-chewed sesame seed

65

on the ground. Howie, ~~who was as sensitive as a~~ who was sensitive, looked the other way. He still thought birds could be pretty gross, but he didn't want Dean to know that. Besides, he had more important things than a half-chewed sesame seed to pay attention to.

"What's that?" he asked.

SSSHHPLLOOSH! SSHHK-WUMPSH! SSSMMURRRSHHH!

There it was again! Except closer this time.

"Help!" a familiar voice cried.

"It's Delilah!" said the keenly keen wire-haired dachshund puppy superhero. "We've got to save her!"

Howie and Dean donned their disguises delaylessly.

Suddenly Delilah burst into the room.

(Luckily, they'd just finished putting on their masks.)

"Stinky Dog! Little D!" Delilah cried out, amazed to see them. "Something's after me! You've got to stop it!"

Howie's nostrils twitched. "P. U.," he said, "you smell as bad as I do."

"Why, thank you, Stinky Dog," Delilah said, swooning and swaying slightly. "It's so kind of you to notice."

"Kind? No, no. Perceptive, perhaps. Sensitive, certainly. Awesomely aware—"

Delilah didn't want to interrupt an alliterative superhero, but she *was* being chased, after all. She hastened to explain. "I was . . . well, I was rolling in the compost heap. I know it's still against the law, but ever since you appeared, Stinky Dog, I've felt called to obey a higher law: the law of stinkiness. Then, out of nowhere, this . . . *thing* appeared!" Delilah shuddered.

"And there it is *now*!" cried Little D.

KEERRAKKK! The wall gave way! **SSHHKWUMPSH! PLOOOFFSSHH!** It appeared! It was too horrible to describe.

So I won't bother.

Howie's Writing Journal

Uncle Harold just looked over my shoulder and said, "It's your job as the author to paint the picture, Howie."

"Am I an author or a painter?" I asked, thinking I was being pretty clever.

Uncle Harold didn't laugh. "You can't say something is too horrible to describe and then not describe it. And, by the way, 'delaylessly' is not a word. You mean, 'without delay.'"

"I was going for alliteration," I said. "It's a style thing."

Uncle Harold suddenly remembered he was needed in the next room. The next room is a closet. I hope he isn't losing his mind.

KEERRAKKK! The wall gave way!

SSHHKWUMPSH! PLOOOFF-SSHH! A creature crashed into the room! It was huge and foamy and so white it was almost blinding! Bubbles kept popping all over its hideously sweet-smelling body! Its big pink eyes seemed to be laughing! Instantly Stinky Dog knew what—no, he knew *who*—it was.

"So we meet at last, B-Man!" he said.

"This is B-Man?" Little D chirped. "But he looks like an overflowing—"

"Exactly," said Stinky Dog. "He looks like an overflowing bathtub. What else would you expect **BATH MAN** to look like?"

Delilah shrieked. Then she fainted.

Bath Man roared with laughter.

"She's mine now!" he bellowed, belching a barrage of bubbles as he did.

Stinky Dog thought really stinky thoughts—so stinky they cannot be printed here for fear of offending the reader and possibly disqualifying the author from Newbony Award consideration for the rest of his career. Trust me, though, these thoughts were *really, really stinky*!

Bath Man laughed even harder. "You've met your match, Stinky Dog!" he said, cackling. **"YAHAHA (BUBBLEBUBBLE) HAHA!"**

Stinky Dog was unable to move. Overpowered by Bath Man's clean-smelling SUPER-SWEETNESS, he watched in horror as Bath Man moved closer and closer until the over-sized, over-sanitized creature bent down and lifted up the passed-out, putrid pooch lying before him.

"Delilah!" Stinky Dog wailed as Bath Man retreated through the broken wall.

"I'll be back," Bath Man warned him. "And next time I'll get you . . . and your little bird, too! **YAHAHA (BUBBLEBUBBLE) HAHA!**"

A bubble burst on the end of Stinky Dog's nose. Bath Man was gone—and so was Delilah.

HOWIE'S WRITING JOURNAL

Now what do I do?!

I had this plan, and then I was writing and I forgot the plan and, well, BATH MAN WASN'T SUPPOSED TO WIN!

What is the point of having a plan if you forget it?

Okay. I still have this chapter in my head where Stinky Dog and Little D go to the Doggie Dimension. But how am I going to get them there? And what about Delilah? I mean, I know who Delilah turns out to be in the end, but she wasn't supposed to faint and get taken away by Bath Man.

I guess I could go back and . . . and . . . revise. But that's so much work. I have a nap scheduled for 3:30. I'd better just keep moving ahead.

CHAPTER 8:
"FIGHT TO THE FINISH"

Stinky Dog had never felt so ashamed in his entire short, superheroic life! Bath Man had just run off with Delilah, the stinkiest dog he'd ever met (other than himself). And as for Little D, his new best friend and loyal side-kick—well, the little fella's face was covered with disappointment. And feathers.

"I'm sorry I let you down, Little D," Stinky Dog said.

"Aw, it's okay, Big D," said Little D. "You couldn't help it. You were immobilized by SUPER-SWEETNESS. I guess it's true what they say—there's nobody more powerful than Bath Man."

Stinky Dog's shame turned into anger! His anger turned into rage! His rage turned into thoughts that were even stinkier than the ones in the last chapter! He could feel a vaporous propulsion of fumes forming under his super-heroic tushy.

"Let's go, Little D!" he commanded.

VVVZZZZOOOMM! Up, up, and away they went!

Below them lay Center City, its citizens no longer afraid to stroll the streets, its little old ladies happily holding their handbags, its canines cavorting in compost—all thanks to Stinky Dog and Little D. But there was still much to be done, a fight that had to be fought to the finish. There were laws still to be changed, corruption still to be revealed, and—most urgently—the evil Bath Man still to be found and sent down the drain! But where was he to be found? Try as he might, Stinky Dog could not detect the smell of sweetness over his own **SUPER-STENCH**.

"Look, Big D!" he heard Little D say.

Stinky Dog looked down. A little old lady was waving her arms at them as if she wanted them to come to her.

"She doesn't look as if she's in trouble," said Stinky Dog, fearful of wasting a moment of precious time. If he didn't get to Bath Man soon, Delilah might lose all her stinkiness and remain sweet-smelling the rest of her life. Stinky Dog shuddered at the thought. Still, there was something about the way the little old lady was waving that seemed important.

"Come on!" he said.

Imagine his surprise to discover that the little old lady was the very first person he had rescued.

"Nice outfit," she commented. "I like the cape and the little panty-things. They're new since I saw you last, aren't they? Not to mention your sidekick. Hello, birdy."

"Chirp," said Little D. His answer seemed to satisfy her.

"I, uh, I don't mean to be rude," said Stinky Dog, "but I've got—"

"Yes, yes, I know," said the little old lady. "You've got to catch Bath Man and save the world from his evil, bubbly ways. I won't keep you."

How did she know about Bath Man? Who *was* this little old lady, anyway?

"Here," she said, digging in her purse. "I have something for you. I have something in here for you, too, dear," she said to Dean, "if you'll just give me a . . . oh, here they are."

She broke off a crumb from a stale roll and placed it in Little D's beak. Then she offered Stinky Dog a chew bone. "I didn't feel I had thanked you enough," she said. "Or even sufficiently."

"Oh, but—"

"Don't eat it right away, dear," she said to

Stinky Dog. She arched her eyebrows. Stinky Dog had watched enough television to know that arched eyebrows meant something. He never knew what they meant, but he knew they meant *something*.

He looked down at the chew bone. There was writing on it:

YOU ARE MORE THAN YOU KNOW

These words were followed by the mysterious, enigmatic, and cryptic message: 18 + 18.

"What does this mean?" Stinky Dog asked.

He looked up. The little old lady was no longer there.

HOWIE'S WRITING JOURNAL

That is the best cliffhanger I've ever written! Uncle Harold will be so proud of me! I'm going to wait to show him until after I've finished the whole book, though. I showed Delilah what I've written, and was that a mistake!

(The answer is yes.)

She said she is never going to speak to me again.

Well, I've heard that one before. Wait until she sees the final chapter. <u>Then</u> we'll see what she has to say.

CHAPTER 9:
"THE DOGGIE DIMENSION
AND THE TRUTH ABOUT DELILAH"

"Where did she go?" Stinky Dog asked.

Little D shrugged. He would have answered, but his mouth was full of a crumb.

"I guess it doesn't matter," Stinky Dog said, looking at the chew bone. "*This* is what she wanted me to know. But what does it mean?"

Little D studied the message on the chew bone. "It means we should go to the corner of Eighteenth Street and Eighteenth Avenue."

"How do you know that?" Stinky Dog asked.

Little D leaned his head in and whispered confidentially, "We have only twelve pages left to tell the story if you—I mean, Howie Monroe—is going to meet the limit his publisher set for him. I thought I'd better move things along."

"Good point," Howie whispered back.

When they got to the corner of 18th and 18th, they found a store called Cozmik Comiks. A clerk waved them in. He arched his eyebrows meaningfully.

"Read this," the clerk said, handing them a comic book.

"I don't think we have enough time," said Stinky Dog.

"Or pages," Little D pointed out.

"Read this," the clerk repeated, arching his eyebrows again, indicating either great significance or a medical condition in need of attention.

Stinky Dog gasped. The comic book was called **SUPERHEROES OF THE DOGGIE DIMENSION**. With his heart in his mouth (it's an expression, but there's no time—or pages—to explain) he opened the comic.

SKWRRRK! THUHDDD!

Stinky Dog and Little D crashed through the wall of reality into a big crystal room that looked like it had been carved out of ice, except it wasn't cold. There were blinking lights everywhere, and a big sign that read:

THE DOGGIE DIMENSION
WHERE YOUR POWER IS UNLEASHED

"Good pun," Stinky Dog commented to Little D.

They were surrounded by giant video-screens filled with giant talking heads.

"Welcome!" one of the heads said. "I am Kaptain K-9 of the Intergalactic Circle of Power Puppies."

"Welcome!" another of the heads said. "I am RoboRover. I am a bionic basset hound!"

"Welcome!" said yet another head. "I am The Drooler!"

A familiar face filled the fourth and final screen. Stinky Dog's jaw dropped.

"Delilah?" he uttered, utterly confused.

"I am the Wise One, the Ultimate Ruler and Superheroic Power of the Doggie Dimension and the Entire Universe," said the giant Delilah-head.

"C-Cooler than seeds," sputtered the spell-bound sparrow.

"But how . . . what . . . who . . . where . . . when . . . why?" queried the curious caped crusader.

The Wise One said, "If you can stop your sputtering and querying, I will tell you everything."

Stinky Dog and Little D stopped their sputtering and querying at once.

"You have been brought back to the place of your birth," Delilah explained.

"I thought I was born in a pile of muck in front of my house in Center City. After all, Chapter Two is called 'The Birth of Stinky Dog,' and I hate to confuse the reader."

"That was the birth of your special

powers," the Wise One explained. "You were born here in the Doggie Dimension. You were sent to live among ordinary dogs and ordinary people so that you might get to know their ways."

"What about ordinary cats?" Stinky Dog asked, thinking of his friend Chester.

"There are no ordinary cats," the Wise One responded.

Stinky Dog nodded. The Wise One really *was* wise.

"But why was I sent to get to know their ways?" the ever curious and inquisitive superhero asked.

"So that you would know how to move among them when the time came for you to use your superpowers and save the world. You have done well. There is but one task left for you to accomplish."

"Bath Man," said Stinky Dog.

"Bath Man," the Wise One repeated.

"But why can't *you* destroy Bath Man?" Stinky Dog asked. "You are wise, not to mention the Ultimate Ruler and Superheroic Power of the Doggie Dimension and the Entire Universe."

"Because—even though I might wish it otherwise—this story is about *you*. It's up to you to save the world. I've tried to help you out."

"The little old lady," Stinky Dog mused.

"One of my many disguises."

"So *that's* why she didn't pass out from my stinkiness! But why did you let your Delilah-self be taken by Bath Man?"

"Silly superhero. So you would have to rescue me and destroy Bath Man."

Stinky Dog hung his head in shame.

"But I failed," he said.

"Not yet," said the Wise One. "You have only to take your thinking in a new direction. Stinky thoughts are not the only ones with power. Sometimes you have to fight bubbles with bubbles. Now go—destroy Bath Man, rescue Delilah, and save the world!"

"Cooler than seeds," Little D said again. Stinky Dog wondered if he was going to start saying it a lot. He supposed he would just have to put it up with it. After all, good sidekicks are hard to find.

CHAPTER 10:
"SWEETS TO THE SWEET"

VVOOOSSHH!

Stinky Dog and Little D sailed through time and space to land directly in front of Bath Man and Delilah.

"YAHAHA (BUBBLEBUBBLE) HAHA!" said Bath Man. Stinky Dog feared he might be as limited in his vocabulary as Little D.

"You can't destroy me with your stinkiness," Bath Man said. "You're washed up,

Stinky Dog. You're going to have to come clean, and I'm just the one to do the job."

"Not so fast, Bath Man! I'm not as dumb as I look." (That wasn't what he meant to say, but, oh, well.) "I know my stinkiness can't destroy you. Stinkiness is what you *need*. Without it, you're down the drain. In fact, if all the world were clean and sweet-smelling, you'd be out of business."

A look of terror appeared in Bath Man's eyes. All Stinky Dog had to do now was think sweet thoughts.

"Rose gardens, spring rain, powdered baby bottoms," Little D prompted. But these words just prompted Bath Man to break into wild, uproarious laughter.

"You think you can destroy me with sweetiepateetie stuff like that. Grow up and fight like *real* superheroes!"

Stinky Dog hit the panic button. What kind of sweet thoughts would work? He had no idea. All he knew was that Delilah was losing her stinkiness. He couldn't let that happen to her! He . . . yes, he loved her! He loved her fluttering eyelashes and her blonde curly ears. He loved the way she played Rip-the-Rag and the way she told him that he didn't know how to write female characters. He loved the twinkle in her eyes and . . .

Bath Man was growing smaller. His bubbles were popping. His eyes were becoming faint. *FIZZZLE!* **POP!** *SSSSSSTT!* SHPLLMURRZZFTGLURBL.

Bath Man was a little puddle on the floor! Stinky Dog tore off his mask!

"Howie!" Delilah gasped. "My hero!"

"This will have to be our little secret," said Howie.

"Of course, my darling," said Delilah, "just as it will be our little secret that I am really the Wise One, the Ultimate Ruler and Superheroic Power of the Doggie Dimension and the Entire Universe."

"Er, right," said Howie.

"Cooler than seeds," said Little D.

The three friends laughed as they walked off into a golden sunset.

THE END

HOWIE'S WRITING JOURNAL

I asked Uncle Harold what he thinks of my story and he said it's terrific, but next time he's going to hide the thesaurus. That Uncle Harold—he's such a kidder.

Delilah loves it! She said it's the best thing I've ever written. "You _finally_ know how to write female characters," she told me. Then she said, "Do you really love me, Howie?"

I was going to remind her that I write

<u>fiction</u>, but when she blinked those long eyelashes at me and tossed those curly blonde ears I found myself asking, "Delilah, will you go out with me?"

"Oh, Howie," she said. "I would love to."

We're meeting at the compost heap at seven.

Life is even better than fiction.

Especially when you're a dog.